Music Player

STORYBOOK™

CONTENTS

Reader's Digest
Children's Books™

Pleasantville, New York • Montréal, Québec • Bath, United Kingdom

WALT DISNEY'S
THE JUNGLE BOOK

Play Song 1

Long ago, in the jungles of India, a wise old panther named Bagheera found a Man-cub crying in a basket. Knowing how dangerous the jungle could be, he took the helpless baby to a family of wolves. The wolf parents were happy to care for the child. The family named him Mowgli, and he lived with the wolves and learned their ways for 10 years.

Mowgli would have stayed with his wolf family. But one day, Shere Khan, the tiger who ruled the jungle and hated all humans, heard

about Mowgli. He decided the Man-cub must be killed before he could grow up to be a dangerous hunter like the other humans. Bagheera thought that it would be best to bring Mowgli to the Man-village where he would be safe. The boy's wolf family sadly agreed. Bagheera took Mowgli and headed out for the Man-village.

Mowgli trusted the wise panther, but he got very upset when Bagheera told Mowgli where they were going. "I don't want to leave the jungle," the boy insisted.

Play Song 2 That night, Mowgli learned just how dangerous the jungle could be. While Bagheera slept, the sly snake, Kaa, entranced the boy with his eyes and coiled himself around Mowgli's body. He was going to make a meal of him! Bagheera awoke just in time and knocked the snake to the ground. "So you still want to stay in the jungle?" Bagheera asked after Kaa had slunk off. But Mowgli didn't want to be anywhere else. The jungle was his home.

The next morning, Mowgli woke early to the sound of an elephant march. *What fun!* he thought. Mowgli got down on all fours and marched along with the herd of elephants.

Play
Song
3
He wasn't paying attention when the elephant leader, Colonel Hathi, bellowed out, "About face!" and Mowgli ran headfirst into the smallest elephant soldier. Colonel Hathi did not like that Mowgli had ruined his parade. Bagheera was annoyed, too. This time, he ordered Mowgli to follow him to the Man-village immediately. But Mowgli refused.

"Fine! You're on your own!" the panther said and left Mowgli by himself.

Play Song 4 Mowgli wasn't alone for long, however. He soon made friends with a big, friendly bear named Baloo. Baloo showed Mowgli all about life's simple pleasures, like getting a good back scratch, finding good food, and floating on one's back in the water. To Mowgli, it was the perfect life!

Things were wonderful until King Louie, the largest of the jungle apes, heard about the Man-cub in the jungle. King Louie sent a pack of monkeys to find Mowgli so that he could learn the secret that only humans knew—the secret of fire. The monkeys swung down from the trees and stole Mowgli off the ground, right in front of Baloo!

Play Song 5

Luckily, Baloo found Bagheera and the two animals came to save Mowgli. Baloo distracted the monkeys by dressing up as an ape himself while Bagheera freed the boy from the ape king.

Now it was more important than ever to bring Mowgli to the village where he would be safe. Even Baloo agreed with Bagheera. But stubborn Mowgli ran off before Bagheera and Baloo could take him. That was just the opening Shere Khan was looking for—Mowgli, alone. As storm clouds moved across the sky, Mowgli hiked through the jungle all by himself.

Play Song 6 Suddenly, Shere Khan appeared before him! The tiger lunged for the boy, ready to kill him. He didn't realize that one of Mowgli's friends had circled back to find him. Baloo arrived just as Shere Khan pounced and he grabbed the

tiger's tail. At that moment, lightning struck the ground, which started a fire nearby. And Mowgli remembered a piece of advice given him by some friendly vultures: that fire was the one thing Shere Khan feared.

Thinking quickly, the boy grabbed a flaming branch and tied it to the tiger's tail. Shere Khan ran off with a shriek, never to be seen again! Now Mowgli was safe. Even better, he didn't need to go to the Man-village anymore.

Mowgli and Baloo cheered and hugged each other happily. That's when Mowgli heard the most beautiful sound. He looked up and saw a pretty girl singing by the water. The girl looked back at him and smiled. Mowgli was instantly mesmerized by the sight and sound of her. As she turned to go back to her village, Mowgli couldn't help but follow her. He stopped to look back at Baloo. He gave his friend a happy shrug and walked toward the beautiful girl and the Man-village. He'd found a new home at last!

WALT DISNEY'S
101
DALMATIANS

Play Song 1

Once upon a time, in a London townhouse, there lived a Dalmatian named Pongo and his human pet Roger. Roger was a songwriter and spent a lot of time at the piano. Pongo was often left on his own.

One spring day, Pongo decided he'd had enough of the bachelor life. It was time Roger and he each found a mate. He spotted the perfect pair through the window—a beautiful Dalmatian and her lovely young woman. Pongo barked until Roger took him to the park, where the females were headed.

Play Song 2

Pongo pulled Roger everywhere looking for the Dalmatian and her pet. At last, he spied them by the pond. Pongo sprang into action, running around them several times until they were entangled in his leash. They lost their balance and fell—*splash!*—into the pond.

Seconds later, Roger and the woman, Anita, climbed out of the pond, laughing like old friends. Pongo smiled at the other Dalmatian, who introduced herself as Perdita. It wasn't long before Roger and Anita married. Pongo and Perdita promised to be with each other forever.

Life became much more enjoyable for Pongo after Perdita, Anita, and their Nanny moved in, especially when Perdita announced she was expecting puppies. The pups were born one stormy night.

Play Song 3

Anita and Nanny helped Perdita while Roger and Pongo waited. At last, Nanny announced: "Fifteen puppies!" Pongo was thrilled! But there was something wrong with the littlest one. It wasn't moving. As Roger held it gently and rubbed it, though, it began to wriggle. It was alive after all!

One evening, when the puppies were a few weeks old, an old schoolmate of Anita's came to call.

Cruella De Vil wanted to buy all of the puppies, but Roger refused. Cruella stormed out in a rage. "You'll be sorry!"

A few nights later, while Pongo and Perdita were walking Roger and Anita, two thieves forced their way into the townhouse and stole all fifteen puppies. The humans were heartbroken!

Roger and Anita went to the police, but Pongo had a different idea.

Play Song 4 "It's up to us to find them," he told Perdita. They sent out their news on the Twilight Bark. Word passed from dog to dog until it reached a barn in the country. There, a sheepdog, a horse, and a cat remembered hearing puppies barking at the De Vil house.

The cat crept over to the house, and what he saw made him gasp. There before him were ninety-nine Dalmatian puppies! And the puppy thieves were being ordered to kill the puppies by none other than Cruella herself, so she could make them into fur coats!

Play
Song
5
While the thieves were busy on the phone, the cat snuck the puppies into a hiding place under the stairs. Meanwhile, Pongo and Perdita had heard the news and were on their way. They reached the house just in time—the puppy thieves had the puppies cornered! Into the house burst Perdita and Pongo, snarling and growling. The adult dogs kept the thieves busy while the cat helped the puppies escape.

The Dalmatians ran through the ice and snow. At last, they found shelter in a dairy barn. The cows let the puppies have fresh milk, and a friendly collie offered the adults a bit of dinner. They didn't know that Cruella and the puppy thieves were on their trail!

Play Song 6
The next morning, a black Labrador brought news: a van would take them home to London! But Cruella, who was searching the streets, kept them from the van.

Pongo got an idea. "Let's all roll in the fireplace soot!" he said. "We'll be disguised as black Labradors!"

They were able to climb into
the van—right in front of Cruella and the thieves.
But Cruella was onto them.

"After them!" she shouted. Cruella and the thieves
chased the van all through the countryside. Finally, the
car crashed into a snowbank. The van—with all the
dogs—sped away to London.

Back in London, Roger and Anita were lonely. Suddenly, they heard familiar barks, and flung open the door. To their surprise, black Labradors scrambled into the room. They were Pongo, Perdita, and the puppies, covered in soot!

Roger and Anita counted one hundred and one Dalmatians in all! They decided to buy a large country house where they could all live happily and comfortably together.

This story is about

Bob, Bet,

the sea,

big fish,

small
fish

and a
magic fish.

3

Bob and Bet live
by the sea.

The fish gives Bob and
Bet three wishes.

"I wish to be rich," says Bob.

"I wish to be richer," says Bet.

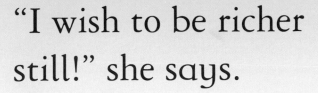

"I wish to be richer
still!" she says.

"Too greedy!"
says the fish.

Puzzles

Which order should
the pictures be in?

Puzzle 1

A   B   C   D

Puzzle 2

A   B   C   D

Puzzle 3

A

B

C

D

Puzzle 4

A

B

C

D

Puzzle 5

Match the words to the picture.

Bet   boots   bird   bones

broom   bowl   Bob

Puzzle 6

What does Bob wish for?

What does Bet wish for?

What would
you wish for?

Answers to puzzles

Puzzles 1-4

ADCB

BCAD

DBCA

ACDB

Puzzle 5

Bob   bones   Bet

bird

bowl

boots   broom